THE QUIZ MASTER

Michael Scott

SHORTLIST

First published in 2004 by
New Island
This Large Print edition published
2011 by AudioGO Ltd
by arrangement with
New Island

ISBN 978 1 4056 2321 6

British Library Cataloguing in Publication Data available

Printed and bound in Great Britain by
MPG Books Group Limited

THE QUIZ MASTER

'And the final question of tonight's quiz is . . .' Harry Evans paused, enjoying his moment of power. The entire pub was hanging on his every word. There were thirty tables set out in the function room with five people to a table, plus the usual hangers-on who had wandered in from the bar.

'Get on with it,' someone shouted from the back of the room.

'Hurry up!'

'Forgotten the question?'

Harry raised his hand for silence. He was short and stout. The long strand of hair that he combed over his bald head reached down to his shoulders. He liked to think that no one noticed. He was mistaken.

Harry made a big production of picking up the last yellow card and adjusting his glasses, though he knew the question by heart. Harry Evans knew all the questions. He had been setting them for pub quizzes around north county Dublin for the past twenty years. Harry liked to consider himself *the* quiz master.

'The final question is: what was the name of the character played by Al Pacino in the 1983 movie *Scarface*?'

A buzz of conversation ran around the long room. In the main body of the pub outside the question was repeated. 'Silence,' Harry called sternly. 'If I hear any conversation, I'll declare the question null and void.'

'What's the question again?' a female voice shouted.

Without referring to the card, Harry repeated the question.

Heads bent over pages. Drinks were quickly forgotten. Most tables had at least one contestant who was a movie buff. On the really good tables, each of the five members was an expert in a different subject: sport, politics, history, movies or general knowledge. Pub-quiz professionals, teams who went from pub to pub around Dublin every weekend playing for small sums of money, took up half the tables in the Blue Swan pub. However, tonight's prize of five thousand euro had brought in players from across the country.

At one of the tables at the back of the hall, Joey Mullins reached for the pencil. 'Brian de Palma,' he said confidently.

'That's the director!' Greg snatched the pencil away from his younger brother. He squeezed his eyes shut, trying to concentrate. 'I should know it. I can see it. Pacino in a white suit.'

'With a scar,' Joey said, chewing the end of the pencil.

'I know he had a scar. That's why it's called *Scarface*.' Greg turned to the third member of the team. 'Spider, what's the answer?' Spider would know. He knew all sorts of trivia, but he was an expert on movies. 'Spider,' Greg hissed again.

Spider wasn't listening. He was staring at the screen of his mobile phone. Mobile phones were forbidden in the function room for the duration of the quiz. He'd forgotten that he had brought his with him until it had buzzed in his pocket a moment ago. He'd pulled it out to turn it off. Naturally he'd glanced at the screen.

ONE MISSED CALL.

He hit the menu button, scrolling to the missed calls.

GILLIAN.

His girlfriend. Spider frowned. Gillian knew he was taking part in the quiz. She knew she shouldn't be calling him.

ONE NEW TEXT MESSAGE.

He should have turned the phone off and shoved it back in his pocket.

Instead he thumbed the message icon and the screen scrolled.

I'M PREGNANT.

Spider looked at the message, frowning. It didn't make sense. He knew what the words meant, but they didn't sink in. He looked up. He could see Greg and Joey looking at him. Their mouths were moving as if they were talking to him, but he couldn't hear the words.

'Hey!'

A shout cut through the low hum of conversation in the room.

'Hey! There's a phone here!' A woman at the next table, wearing too much eye shadow and thick lipstick, was pointing to them. 'They're using a phone.'

The room fell silent.

'Disqualified,' Harry Evans announced immediately. 'Unless you're a doctor on call, phones are expressly forbidden.' Harry stood—which didn't increase his height much—and frowned over the top of his glasses at the three young men sitting at the table. 'And you lads don't look like doctors to me. Disqualified!'

'Hey, are you suggesting we're cheating?' Joey stood and glared at Harry Evans. Joey Mullins stood six foot two in his stocking feet and was built in proportion.

Greg reached up to lay a hand on his brother's arm. 'Leave it.'

Harry took a quick drink to wet his suddenly dry throat. 'I'm suggesting no such thing. But the rules of entry are very clear: no mobile phones in the room.' Over the past few years, phones had become the bane of the pub-quiz scene.

'We paid a hundred euro for this table . . .' Joey looked around the room. Himself, Greg and Spider were probably the youngest people there. He could see no support.

'And you agreed to abide by the rules,' Harry said, more confidently now. He could see the bouncers in their black suits gathering at the rear of the room.

Greg stood. He was a few inches shorter than his younger brother, though he was as broad. Like Joey, he wore his hair shaved close to his skull. He was only too aware of the image they projected. 'You are perfectly right,' he said. 'We've just got a call from home. From our mother. Who is ill,' he added.

'She's not, is she?' Joey looked shocked.

Greg's fingers tightened on his brother's arm, silencing him.

'I'm sorry to hear that, but rules are rules,' Harry said. 'I'll have to ask you to leave.'

Joey opened his mouth, but Greg squeezed his arm again, harder this time. 'We'll be off,' he said. He turned and caught Spider by the wrist, dragging him to his feet.

Spider looked at him blankly. 'What?' he asked.

'We're off,' Greg said. Holding

Spider by one arm and his brother by the other, he marched towards the door. The four black-suited bouncers parted, two on either side, as they approached.

'Smart move boys,' one of them said.

'We could have taken you,' Joey said loudly, glaring at him.

The night air outside was sharp and clear after the heavy heat of the room. Greg finally let go of the others' arms. He spun Spider around to face him. 'Tell me,' he said.

Spider looked at Greg. He was Greg's height but slender and dark, almost Spanish looking. He wore his long hair pulled back into a tight pony-tail. On the back of his left hand, in the web of skin between his thumb and index finger, he had the tattoo of the spider that gave him his nickname. Spider dropped his phone into Greg's beefy hand.

Frowning, Greg looked at the screen then scrolled the message.

He sucked in a deep breath. 'Her father's going to kill you.'

'What's wrong?' Joey demanded.

'Gillian's pregnant.'

Joey nodded. 'Oh yeah, her da will kill you. And don't forget her brothers. Her two big brothers. Who do martial arts.'

Greg wrapped his arm around his friend's shoulder as they walked to his car. 'You'll think of something. You need to talk to Gillian before making any decisions.'

Spider nodded. 'Hey, I'm sorry about the quiz. I'd just seen the message and I wasn't thinking . . .'

'Don't worry about it. There'll be other quizzes,' Greg said.

'I'll make it up to you, pay you back the money.'

'I know you will,' Greg said.

'There's just one thing I want to know,' Joey said, as he climbed into the car.

Greg and Spider turned to look at him.

'What *was* the name of the character played by Al Pacino in *Scarface*?'

'Tony Montana,' Spider said immediately.

2

Spider waited until the Mullins had disappeared into the night, their red tail-lights flaring, before he started walking towards the house. He fished his mobile phone from his pocket and held it tightly in his hand.

There were forty-two steps from the corner of the road to Gillian's gate. There were ten from her gate to her hall door.

Spider noticed such things. He had a head for trivia—useless snippets of information. He knew that Element Four had composed the theme tune to the *Big Brother* series. He knew that Stanley Matthews, playing for Blackpool, had won European Footballer of the Year in 1956. Ronaldo of Real Madrid won it in 2002. The European Cup Winner's Cup was established in 1960 . . .

Spider took a deep breath and

tried to calm his hammering heart. He slowed as he approached the gate that led to Gillian's house.

He had a habit of running through his banks of trivia when he was upset or agitated. And right now, he was both.

Gillian was pregnant. He didn't know how that had happened. Well, actually he did. They had gone off for a weekend together three months ago—three months and ten days to be precise. They'd had a fabulous time.

Although she was eighteen, this was the first time she'd managed to get away from the watchful eyes of her parents and her two overly protective brothers. None of them thought Spider was good enough for her. She'd said she was staying with a girlfriend, but they'd spent the weekend together in West Cork.

And now she was pregnant.

They had talked about getting married. There had never been any real doubts. It was something they both wanted to do. All they needed was money and a place of their own. Right now they had neither. Gillian was a student, still living at home with her parents. Spider worked part time in the garage with Greg Mullins, being paid just above minimum wage. He occasionally got paid under the counter and had managed to put away nearly a thousand euro. He was going to college at night, taking a car-maintenance course. But he knew that he needed to make a serious decision about his future.

Well, now it looked as if the decision had been made for him.

There was no doubt in his mind that he was going to look after Gillian and the baby. He had known her for most of his life. They had started out as friends, but over the past year the relationship had become deeper.

When they had discussed marriage it was always in some distant future.

They'd do it when he was settled with a job, she had a career and they had a house of their own. Without a place of their own there was no way they could get married. It would mean moving in with Gillian's parents. And her mother and father hated Spider. They thought he was a waster, a good-for-nothing in a dead-end job with no prospects and no future.

Sometimes even Spider had to agree with them.

Spider enjoyed the fantasy of turning up at Gillian's home one day in a fancy new car, wearing a tailor-made suit and holding the keys to the new house he had just purchased. Then Gillian's parents would have no excuse to keep them apart. Technically, of course, her parents couldn't prevent them from marrying. She was eighteen and he was nineteen. They were both over the age of consent. But her parents could—and did—make things very difficult. Gillian's father—a huge bear of a man—had threatened Spider with physical violence only the previous week. Spider had no doubts that the man meant it.

Spider stopped. He was standing in the shadow of the tall hedge surrounding Gillian's home. The hedge was shaped into a perfect box, and there was a scattering of leaves on the ground. He breathed deeply. The sharp, slightly bitter scent of greenery hung in the night air. Gillian's mother must have trimmed the hedge earlier.

Spider peered through the hedge. He could just make out Gillian's bedroom window through the leaves. One corner of the curtains was bright, indicating that she had her bedside light on. Spider glanced at his watch: ten minutes to midnight. He thumbed his mobile phone. He would have to text Gillian. If she didn't have her phone set to silent, ringing might wake the whole house.

R U AWAKE?

A couple of seconds passed before his screen blinked orange.

WAITING FOR YOU.

CAN YOU TALK?

NO.

HAVE YOU TOLD THEM?

NOT YET.

WHEN CAN WE TALK?

TOMORROW AFTER COLLEGE, I'LL BE AT THE USUAL PLACE.

The light in the bedroom went off. Spider waited a second, then tapped in a last message.

IT'LL WORK OUT. I PROMISE. I LOVE YOU.

But there was no response.

3

'The team from The Bridge social club won the quiz last night,' Greg said quietly. He was staring into the engine of a battered ten-year-old Mazda 626. Not looking at Spider, who was standing beside him, he added, 'Apparently the last question stumped everyone.'

Spider knelt in front of the car and ran his hand under the radiator. It came away wet and sticky. 'Rad is gone. I'm surprised this car is still running.'

'No one knew the answer.' Greg continued as if he hadn't heard. 'I was talking to Tony, down at The Bridge Garage. He was there last night. Eventually one of his team guessed it, but it was only a guess.'

Spider straightened and pressed his dirty hands into the small of his back, rubbing them on his overalls.

'I know what you're trying to do.' He smiled.

'Do—me? What am I trying to do?' Greg asked, returning to the engine. He pulled over a high-powered torch and shone it into the engine. 'Hmm, I'll bet the manifold is gone too.'

'You're trying to distract me,' Spider said. 'I've seen you do it with Joey when he's in a humour.'

Greg turned to look at his friend. 'Well, at least you recognise that you're in a humour. You turn up here half an hour late with a face like thunder. You don't say a word to anyone. And I think you've dropped every tool you've taken up.'

'I'm sorry, Greg. It's just . . .'

'I know,' Greg said. 'Did I ever tell you about the time my Tricia thought she was pregnant?' He lowered his voice and glanced over at his brother. Joey had a big heart, but he had a mouth to match. 'We'd been going out with one another for about

18

a year. One day she announced she was pregnant. I didn't know what to do or where to go. Finally we decided that we'd tell her family. Luckily I didn't have her da to contend with, but I'd got to face her ma. And you know what she's like.'

Spider grinned. Tricia Collins' mother was a tiny woman but with a terrifying reputation. 'What happened?'

'We were in the kitchen, chatting to the ma, which was how we'd rehearsed it. Then, casually, Tricia slipped it into the conversation. 'So ma,' she said, 'I've got some great news for you. You're going to be a granny after all.''

Spider's grin widened.

'Without saying a word, without batting an eyelid, her ma whacked me across the head with the first thing that came to hand. It happened to be a plate of chicken curry. The plate bounced off my thick skull, but I was picking curry out of my ears

19

for weeks. That was the first time I shaved my head,' he added. 'No matter how often I washed my hair I could still smell curry from it. I've never been fond of curry since.'

Spider was laughing so hard now tears were rolling down his cheeks.

'That's better,' Greg said. 'It's good to see you smiling again. And you know something else? Tricia was wrong. It was a false alarm.'

Spider suddenly looked hopeful. 'You think?'

Greg shrugged. 'I don't know. I'm just saying wait until you've a bit more information before you decide on a course of action.'

Spider nodded. 'Thanks, Greg. I appreciate it.' He turned back to the engine and began to work on the manifold. 'You know I love her,' he said, his voice echoing slightly from beneath the bonnet.

'I know that.'

'And we will get married.'

'I know that too.'

Spider eased off the manifold. Thick black dust curled up. He pulled back, coughing. 'This car has never been serviced.'

'You were about to ask me for the afternoon off,' Greg continued.

Spider stopped. 'How did you know?'

'Because you didn't get a chance to talk to Gillian last night, and she's out of college in an hour. It's my guess you've arranged to meet her.' He paused. 'Take whatever time you need.'

Spider wiped his hands on an oily rag. 'Thanks Greg. You're all right, you know that?'

'I'm too soft, that's what I am. Go on. Take your timc. You're useless to me here.'

Spider walked away smiling.

*   *   *

Spider didn't know where most of the things he knew came from. He walked along the banks of the canal, scattering crumbs of bread into the dark water. In his wake he left a long line of grumbling ducks. He'd always had a memory for trivia. One of his earliest memories was of lying in bed in the grotty flat he'd lived in when his parents were alive. It was a two-bedroom flat, but they'd converted a cupboard into a third bedroom for him. It was so narrow that a bed would not fit in. He had to sleep in a sleeping-bag on the floor. He could remember clearly lying in the sleeping-bag and counting the cracks in the plasterwork in the ceiling. And he could still remember the exact number of cracks.

He knew that trivia was an escape for him. It was an escape from parents who spent every night in the pub and returned home drunk and loud, who often fought with screams and shouts—and occasionally slaps and punches. He'd wake in the morning to find his mother with a split lip or his father with a black eye. He supposed they loved one another. He was never sure. They fought like cats and dogs with each other, but woe betide anyone who said anything against either of them.

His sister Ellie had the second bedroom. She was nearly fifteen years older than Spider. Growing up, he'd been aware that she was a beauty. She left when he was about ten to go to London and model. There were Christmas cards in the beginning, but it had been years since he'd last heard from her. Someone had told him she'd been married, divorced and married again.

Ellie had been kind to the shy little boy when she'd lived at home. But once she had left he had retired into his own world. It was a world where little things meant a lot, where his knowledge about things—no matter how trivial—gave him a certain amount of power.

Now all he had to do was to see or

hear something just once and it stuck with him.

He knew that there were twenty-one ducks in the water behind him. He knew that one had a broken foot and that another had a splash of white on the tip of its beak. He knew that it was three hundred steps from one bridge to the other, that there was one park bench—with a rotten seat—one rubbish bin and one lifebuoy post without the red lifebuoy in it.

Spider stopped. He forced himself to breath deeply.

This trivia was driving him mad. It was also preventing him from concentrating on the real question. If Gillian was pregnant, what was he going to do?

4

'I think my mum suspects,' Gillian said, falling into step beside Spider.

'So . . .' He sucked in a breath. 'So, you're sure yourself. I mean, you're sure—'

'I'm sure I'm pregnant,' Gillian snapped. 'Yes, I'm sure.' She took a deep breath and placed her hand on Spider's arm. 'I'm sure.'

They walked on in silence, then darted across the busy main road and cut through a little gate that led into St Stephen's Green. Gillian was doing a post-leaving-certificate course in a college off the green. Her father said he thought eighteen was too young to enter university. But Gillian knew he really thought she was too immature.

After the buzz of traffic, the silence in the huge park was a relief. Noises became distant, filtered through the rustling of the trees. Faint and high on the air came the voices of children playing, their cries like the calls of exotic birds.

Gillian slipped her arm through Spider's, closed her eyes and turned her face to the sun coming through the trees. She was almost as tall as Spider and was dark haired and dark eyed like him. She inhaled deeply. The metallic taste of the traffic was replaced with the richer smells of life and growth. When she opened her eyes again she looked at Spider. He was turned away from her, staring across the park to where a young couple were playing with a toddler. The child was wobbling in circles, chasing a brightly coloured ball.

'It comes down to this,' he said suddenly. 'Do you love me?'

The question took her by surprise. She opened her mouth to make an instant response, then stopped. This was too important a question for a snap answer. It was also the first time she'd been forced to really think about it. Did she love Spider?

Slowly, decisively Gillian nodded. Yes. Yes, she did love him. He was kind and gentle, funny and awkward, and she loved him for that. 'Yes,' she said.

'Good.' Spider smiled, and when he did his whole face lit up. 'I love you too. You know that.'

Although it wasn't a question, Gillian nodded.

'And the next question is: do we want this child?'

Gillian looked away. The flower-beds in the green were in full bloom. The hot, wet summer had brought out the best in them. This year the colours werc mostly white and blue. In the middle of one of the flower-beds a gardener was delicately weeding between the spots of colour.

'Gillian?'

She'd thought about this all week. She'd thought about nothing else since she'd first suspected, then confirmed, that she was pregnant. She had even taken a page from her copy book, drawn a line down the middle and written down the pros and cons of the situation. There were more cons than pros. She was too young. They had nowhere to live. They had no money. Her parents would kill her. How would she be able to continue school and then university? Her parents hated Spider . . .

All the negatives jumbled together into a huge mess, until it became clear to her that she could not have this child. To do so would be to ruin her life and her future.

And yet . . .

And yet it was her baby, hers and Spider's. Despite all the negatives, she knew she wanted it. She took a deep breath. 'I want to keep the baby, Spider.'

The young man nodded. He guessed that would be the answer. 'We need to tell your parents,' he said. 'We need to let them know.' He glanced sideways at her. 'You said you think your mum suspects?'

Gillian nodded. 'I've caught her watching me carefully. Every morning she lingers outside the bathroom, or she'll be in her bedroom with the door open. I know she's listening. And I don't know how many times recently she's asked me if I'm feeling OK.'

'What do you think will happen when she tells your dad?'

Gillian suddenly looked fearful. 'I think he'll go mad. He'll want to kill you.'

Spider nodded. 'That's what I was afraid of.' He tried to sound macho and unconcerned but failed. 'He really hates me, doesn't he?'

'I'm his little girl. He wants the best for me,' Gillian said. She squeezed Spider's arm. 'He just doesn't realise that I want you.'

The couple walked across the little bridge and turned left, heading for

Grafton Street.

'Here's what we will do,' Spider said. 'We'll wait until your father is out and then talk to your mother together. We'll tell her what's happened and see if she can help. I don't think she dislikes me,' he added.

Gillian nodded. 'She doesn't *dislike* you. Of course, that was before . . .'

'Before?'

'Before you got me pregnant.'

They walked under the huge arched entrance to the park and waited at the lights at the top of Grafton Street.

'When would be a good time to do it?'

Gillian thought. 'Tonight. Dad will be driving the boys to training. Then he'll hang around until they're finished. We'll have an hour and a half before he's home.'

Spider swallowed hard and nodded decisively. 'Tonight it is then.'

5

Greg Mullins sat in his usual seat at the back of the pub and listened intently to Spider. Tricia, his long-time on-off girlfriend was sitting beside him. She was sipping a Bloody Mary and texting furiously.

'I think you're doing the right thing,' Greg said. 'What do you think, Tricia?'

She grunted, eyes fixed on the small screen. 'Absolutely,' she said.

Spider stared at the Coke on the table in front of him. Greg had bought the first round of drinks. Spider knew he should offer to get the next round in, but he'd only enough for the bus fare to Gillian's home. He wasn't even sure if he'd enough to get back to his flat above the garage.

'What advice can you give Spider?' Greg asked Tricia.

Tricia looked uncomfortable. She sipped her drink and shrugged. 'It's not going to be easy. Her ma will go hysterical, so you've got to be prepared for that.' She paused and took another sip. 'I suppose you're going to offer to marry Gillian?'

'Of course!'

Tricia shook her head. 'Big mistake. That's the last thing they want to hear. They won't want to know that their daughter is marrying—' She suddenly stopped. Her cheeks were touched with colour.

'A waster,' Spider finished with a smile. 'I know.'

'The only piece of advice I can give you is to get in and out before the da comes home,' Greg said. 'Tell you what. You're seeing her at what time?'

'Seven thirty.'

'How long should the conversation take?'

'Five minutes,' Tricia giggled. 'But

32

it will seem like an hour.'

'I'll pull up in the van around eight and wait just down the road,' Greg went on. 'So if you need to do a legger, you'll know where to find me.'

'I'm not running away,' Spider said indignantly.

'If I saw old-man Bradley coming at me I'd run away,' Greg laughed. 'He's huge, and those two lads of his are even bigger.'

Spider finished the last of his Coke in one long swallow. He could feel it hit the pit of his stomach and turn sour. 'Thanks,' he whispered.

*   *   *

The bus was late.

Spider stood at the bus stop on the quays and watched bus after bus sail by. Some of them were full but most had 'Out of Service' showing in the little window across the front. He glanced at his cheap digital watch.

Five past seven. And it was at least a thirty-minute bus journey out to Swords. He was going to be late.

Another bus chugged by, this one trailing a cloud of filthy fumes. The side of the bus had an ad for *Kwizzers*, the quiz show that had been running on TV for the past eight weeks.

The show had taken the country by storm. In its simplest form it was another pub quiz but with harder questions and bigger prizes. Before it had even come into the country there had been a six-week radio and TV advertising blitz. Very recently someone had just won the one million pound prize in Britain. 'Seven steps to heaven' was its tag line. There were only seven questions in the quiz. The first question was worth one euro, the second question was worth ten euro and every question after that was worth ten times more. The prize for the seventh question was one million euro. There was no element of chance in the game. It took simply a combination of skill and general knowledge. Even getting onto the game required answering a series of questions on a premium-rate phone call. But that didn't stop thousands trying every week. The show was then broadcast live at prime time on Saturday night.

The bus arrived, and the doors hissed open. Spider was first in the queue, but he was roughly pushed out of the way by an old woman carrying a shopping bag almost as big as herself. 'I was here first, sonny,' she snapped. She heaved herself up onto the bus, then turned to glare at Spider. 'Did you see that?' she said to the driver. 'He wouldn't even help an old woman. The youth of today!'

The driver nodded and winked at Spider. 'The youth of today,' he agreed. 'It's a pity their elders aren't around to show them a better example.'

The old woman squinted at the bus driver, unsure if he was getting at her or not. She flashed her bus pass and clattered down to the back of the bus.

'Ignore her,' the driver said as Spider climbed on board. 'She does that every night. You're lucky. Usually she's carrying a walking-stick, and she's not afraid to use it.'

Spider climbed the stairs and sat at the back of the bus. He stared down into the murky waters of the Liffey. He was rehearsing how he would begin his conversation with Gillian's mother.

'Mrs Bradley, I'm sorry to tell you . . .'

No, he couldn't say that. It made it sound as if he was apologizing.

'Mrs Bradley, Gillian and I would like to tell you . . .'

No, he couldn't say that either. That made it look as if he was hiding behind Gillian's name.

'Mrs Bradley, we're delighted to

tell you . . .'

But they weren't delighted.

'Mrs Bradley, you know Gillian and I have been seeing one another for a while now. We love one another. And we're going to have a baby.'

Spider took a deep breath. This was not going to be easy.

6

At precisely seven forty-two, Spider licked his suddenly dry lips and pressed his finger on the gleaming doorbell.

He'd made an effort with his appearance. He'd washed his over-long hair, brushed it until it shone and pulled it back off his face in a pony-tail. He was wearing his best pair of black jeans, his black boots and a black T-shirt. There was a hole in the T-shirt under the arm, but he had no plans to take off his black leather jacket so he reckoned no one would notice.

Deep in the house, the bell played a chirpy 'Whistle While You Work'.

Spider risked a quick glance at his mobile. He'd tried phoning Gillian on the way over, but his calls had gone straight to her message machine. There had been no texts from her.

A shape moved in the hall. He could see it approach through the frosted glass. He fixed a smile on his face.

A lock turned, the door opened . . .

*   *   *

Mrs Bradley knew what was wrong the moment she saw Spider O'Brien standing on her doorstep. All the little clues of the past few weeks fell into place. Gillian's moodiness, loss of appetite, trips to the bathroom and colour and appearance in the morning now made sense.

The woman looked at the young man standing on the doorstep, in his scuffed leather jacket and jeans, and knew that he had got her daughter pregnant.

She looked at him.

And then she screamed.

*   *   *

39

'She screamed?' Greg asked, frowning. 'She didn't say anything? She just screamed?'

Spider nodded. He was sitting in Greg's van, slumped against the door. He raised a can of Coke to his lips and was embarrassed when he realised that his fingers were still shaking. 'You never heard anything like it. It was terrifying.'

'And what did you do?'

'I ran,' Spider said. 'I turned and ran.'

Greg cracked open a can and took a deep swallow. 'I'd have done the same myself,' he said. 'What did Gillian say?'

Spider took out his phone. Even though it was showing no missed calls and no messages, he still checked. 'She's saying nothing,' he said. 'I can't get through to her at all.' He turned to look at his friend. 'What do I do, Greg—what do I do?'

Greg Mullins shook his head. 'I

40

don't know,' he said. 'I just don't know.'

*   *   *

Gillian sat in the centre of the sofa and flicked channels on the TV. She wasn't looking at the picture and had the sound turned down. She could hear her mother talking urgently with her father. Gillian couldn't make out the words, but she didn't need to. She knew what her mother was saying.

Gillian had been upstairs in her bedroom when Spider had rung the doorbell. She'd been about to come downstairs when she heard her mother scream.

She had never heard a sound quite like it. It was a cross between terror and rage, an animal outpouring of emotion. She'd dashed from her bedroom and almost tumbled down the stairs, but by that stage Spider was gone. She just caught sight of him running down the drive. Her mother was standing in the hallway, pale faced, her hands pressed to her chest, breathing deeply.

Gillian didn't know what to think. Was her mother having a heart attack? But surely Spider hadn't told her in the hallway.

Sarah Bradley turned to look at her daughter. She drew in a deep breath, and when she spoke her voice was surprisingly calm. 'It's true then. You are pregnant by this . . . this *boy*.' She made the word sound like something foul.

Gillian was surprised by how calm her own voice sounded. 'Yes, I'm carrying Spider's child.' Then she went into the sitting-room and turned on the TV.

Ten minutes later, her father's car had roared into the driveway. Gravel crunched and sprayed as he hit the brakes too hard. Gillian heard the patter of her mother's feet as she ran down the hall and the front door being wrenched open. There were muffled voices, which faded as Sarah brought her husband in to the kitchen. They'd been there ever since.

Gillian flicked to one of the music channels and brought the sound up.

And then the door opened, and her father stepped into the room.

Roy Bradley looked like a prize-fighter, but he was actually a bank manager. He stood six foot six in his socks and, courtesy of a six-year stint in the army, was built in proportion. He wore his iron-grey hair cropped close to his skull. His temper was legendary. Right now he was calm, almost dangerously so.

Roy crossed the room in a couple of quick strides, lifted the remote control off the arm of the chair and turned off the TV. He sank in his recliner facing Gillian and leaned forward, resting his elbows on his knees. Then he pushed the palms of both hands together—almost as if he was praying—and pressed the tips of his fingers to his lips. He stared at his daughter with his cold grey eyes, and for a moment Gillian thought she saw a tear there.

'Is it true?'

Gillian could feel her own tears start then, pricking at the back of her eyes. She swallowed hard. 'Yes, it's true.'

Roy nodded.

'Did he . . . did he attack you? Force himself on you?'

Gillian shook her head. 'No, Dad. Spider's not like that.'

Sarah came into the room but hung back, leaning against the wall, watching but not saying anything.

'How many months?'

Gillian had never heard her father speak so softly. 'Three months, I think.'

Roy nodded. 'When you went down to West Cork. You lied to us, told us you were staying with a girlfriend . . .' he began, then stopped. 'And you're sure he didn't force you, didn't spike your drink?'

'I told you he's not like that.'

Roy looked unconvinced.

'Maybe he got drunk.'

'He doesn't drink.'

Her father sat back into the leather chair. It hissed and sighed around him. 'So there's no excuse.'

'Dad, I'm eighteen—' Gillian began.

'He's older.'

'A year. Dad . . . look. We went away together. We went to bed together. We weren't careful. I'm pregnant.'

'What happens now?' Roy asked.

'Spider wants to marry me.'

Roy snorted. 'Over my dead body! He's a lazy good-for-nothing. He has no job, no prospects, no money. You're going to give up everything you've got for that? I don't think so!'

'Dad!'

'Roy!' Sarah added sharply.

Roy Bradley calmed himself. He

looked around the sitting-room. It was decorated in the best of taste, elegant but comfortable. The suite was leather. The carpet was a luxurious, thick pile. The TV was the latest in thirty-six-inch flat screen ... And then the room faded, and he could suddenly see his daughter, his beautiful, only girl, in a squalid bed-sit with a threadbare mat over bare floorboards, mould growing on the walls and a tiny black-and-white TV stuck in the corner.

'Let's just take a moment to think,' Roy said evenly. 'There is no way you can bring up a baby and continue your studies.'

'I'm not having an abortion!'

Roy and Sarah were shocked. They hadn't even considered that.

'Did the boy want you to have an abortion?' Roy's voice was rising.

'He never mentioned it,' Gillian said.

'So you'll have your baby and we'll look after it,' Roy continued. He attempted a smile, which failed. 'It'll be good to have a baby in the house again, won't it?' he asked his wife. Sarah managed a nod and a smile, but it was strained and unconvincing.

'So you'll have the baby, and we'll raise it here. You can then continue with your schooling and university and concentrate on your exam results.'

'What about Spider?'

'Spider? What about him?'

'Well, where does he come in?'

Roy Bradley's smile was grim. 'Oh, he doesn't.'

'But it's Spider's baby too. He wants to be involved.'

'That's what he tells you now, but believe me, when the reality sinks in you'll not see him again.'

Gillian felt her stomach heave. Although she truly believed that Spider loved her, at the very back of her mind, in that dark place where all the horrible thoughts lurked, she couldn't help but think the same thing.

'I know his type,' her father continued. 'Right now he's promising you the sun, moon and stars. But if you think about it he's not in a position to offer you anything. Is he?'

Gillian's stomach heaved again. She lurched out of the chair and barely made it to the downstairs loo before she threw up. She knew her father was right.

7

'You!'

Two incredibly strong hands picked Spider up by the shoulders and flung him across the floor of the garage. He hit the ground hard, then slid on a greasy patch into a display of oil cans. They crashed to the ground around him. One burst open, its thick contents puddling around Spider's feet.

Roy Bradley strode across the floor towards Spider. The big man's face was a mask of rage and hatred.

And then Joey Mullins stepped into his path. Joey was as tall as Roy, though not so broad, but he was thirty years younger. He was also holding a long wheel brace in his hands. 'Enough of that!'

'Get out of my way,' Roy snapped. 'The boy and I are going to have a few words.'

Holding the wheel brace in his right hand, Joey started tapping it against the palm of his left hand. 'Whatever you have to say to him, you can say it here and now. But you'll stay right where you are.'

'What's going on here?' Greg appeared out of the office. He saw Spider on the ground and Joey facing up to an enraged Roy Bradley. Wiping his hands on a cloth, Greg came out onto the floor of the garage and put a hand on his younger brother's shoulder. Then he took the wheel brace away from him. 'No need for that,' he said evenly. He flung it across the room. It clattered off the concrete floor. The noise broke the spell. Suddenly both Roy and Joey looked embarrassed.

'Now, Mr Bradley, what can we do for you?'

Roy took a deep, shuddering breath. 'Greg.' He nodded towards Spider. 'I suppose you've heard there's been a little trouble with the boy.'

'Trouble?' Greg looked shocked. 'What sort of trouble?'

'Don't play the innocent with me,' Roy snapped. 'I suppose he's been down the pub, boasting that he's got my daughter pregnant.'

'No, he hasn't. I do know he's been making plans for the future,' Greg said. 'Now do you want to tell me what you're doing here?'

'I'm here for a chat.'

'What sort of chat?'

'The sort a father has with the man who has got his daughter pregnant.'

'The sort that involves fists?' Greg asked, smiling coldly.

Roy Bradley stabbed a finger into Greg's broad chest. 'What would you do if someone did that to your little girl?'

Greg glanced over his shoulder at Spider. He knew what he'd do: exactly what Roy Bradley was planning to do. He turned back to Roy and forced a smile to his lips. 'They're both over the age of consent, Roy. They were just doing what young people do.'

'That's my little girl you're talking about. She never went out with anyone before him. She's innocent. He's taken that innocence.'

'Maybe we should let them sort out their own problems,' Greg said. 'Get them together, see what sort of future they want for themselves.'

'You're supporting him!' Roy shouted.

Greg sighed. 'I'm trying to run a business. Right now you're stopping me from doing that.'

'I approved your loan for this business,' Roy snapped. 'And don't you forget that!'

Greg looked as if he was going to reply, but he bit back his answer.

Roy looked over at Spider. 'I'm here to tell you that my daughter wants nothing more to do with you. You've had your fun. Now she has to live with the consequences for the rest of her life.' Roy deliberately kept his voice even and low. 'I'd such hopes for her—a good education, travel, a career, a good husband when the time was right, then children. But you've ruined all that.'

'I think you're being a little dramatic,' Greg began.

'You keep your nose out of this! This is none of your business.'

Spider staggered to his feet. His head was ringing. His left shoulder and arm were numb. 'Gillian and I want to be together,' he said. His voice shook at first, then settled and became stronger. 'We're going to be married. I'll be proud to be a father to the child.'

Bradley's face turned into a mask of contempt. 'You! And what could you offer my daughter? You've no home, no money, no future. You have nothing. You *are* nothing!'

Then he turned and walked towards the door. He stopped just before he stepped into the yard

and looked back at Greg. 'I won't
forget this next time you come to me
looking for a loan.'

*   *   *

Spider sat in the tiny main office,
a mug of steaming tea on the desk
before him. His shirt was off. Joey
was squeezing and twisting his left
arm.

'I don't think anything is broken,'
he said. Joey did karate three times
a week. He had recently taken up
a first-aid course to help with the
minor injuries he and others suffered
during class.

Greg sat on the other side of
the battered desk, a cup of tea
untouched in his hand. 'I suppose
you could bring a charge of assault
against him.'

Spider laughed, but it hurt his
shoulder and he stopped. 'I don't
think so, do you?'

Greg shook his head. 'Probably

not a good idea to bring a charge of assault against your future father-in-law.'

'I'm sorry I've got you involved. Can he hurt the business?'

Greg considered for a moment, then shook his head. 'Once, maybe. Not now. There are lots of banks, lots of bank managers. Besides, I was thinking of changing banks anyway.' He grinned. 'We'll take our business away from him, rather than the other way around.'

Spider stood and worked his shoulder from side to side. 'Feels better.' He flexed the fingers of his left hand. They all worked. 'I want to thank you both for standing up for me. God only knows what he would have done if you hadn't been here.'

Joey nodded. 'It's not over though. You'll have to watch out for Gillian's brothers. They're mean fellas. We had to ask them to leave the karate club a couple of months ago.'

Greg stood, lifted his cup and

drained it in one quick swallow. 'Come on, Joey. Let's get some work done. Spider, you sit here for a while and drink your tea. Let the feeling come back into that arm.'

Greg and Joey stepped out of the tiny office, pulling the door closed behind them. Something about Greg's expression bothered Spider. As soon as the door closed he got to his feet, crossed the room and pressed his ear against the flaking wood. He could hear fragments of conversation.

'There's going to be trouble.' Greg's voice was serious. 'Bradley can hurt us.'

'Spider's our friend—'

'Spider's an employee who, right now, is in deep water with the man who holds the purse strings of this garage.'

Joey's voice was hard. 'So what are you going to do?'

'What am I going to do? I might have to let Spider go.'

'I think you're wrong!'

'If it's any consolation, I think I'm wrong too. But it's our future I'm thinking of. Spider's a bright boy. He'll find his own way.'

'It's not right, not right at all . . .' Joey's voice faded as the two men walked across the floor.

Spider returned to the table and sank back into the chair. He placed both elbows on the table and rested his head in his hands. What a mess. How had things disintegrated so quickly? Only the night before last everything had been good. They'd been at the pub quiz. They were going to win the five thousand euro. He was going to take Gillian off on a real holiday with his share of the winnings.

He felt tears pricking the back of his eyes and angrily blinked them away. The last time he'd cried had been when he'd learned that his parents had been killed in that terrible car crash. It had been

New Year's Day, very early in the morning, and both had been nearly three times over the limit. He'd cried when he watched the two coffins being lowered into the ground. He'd cried when he dropped a handful of the cold, hard clay onto the wood far below. And he'd never cried since.

Spider took a deep breath. He sipped the tea. Joey had added about three spoonfuls of sugar so the tea was sweet and sticky.

There was a newspaper on the table in front of him. Absently, Spider opened it, scanning the headlines, checking the sports results, glancing at his horoscope.

'Today is a good day for making plans . . .'

There's a surprise, he thought.

There was a *Kwizzers* ad at the bottom of page three.

'Phone 10-10-100, answer three questions and you could be in with a chance to appear on this week's *Kwizzers*—seven steps to heaven and the one million euro prize.'

Spider grinned. What he could do with one million euro! There'd be no way Roy Bradley could keep him away from Gillian then. A million would buy them a house, give them and the child a great start in life. The phone number was a premium number costing one euro a minute. Calls should not last longer than four minutes, he read. Four euro. Spider dug in his pocket and pulled out a five euro note. He slid it under Greg's cup. Then he picked up the phone.

8

The number was engaged.

Spider dialled again.

It was still engaged.

One last try. He hit redial.

'Welcome to *Kwizzers*, the one million euro quiz. Are you ready to take seven steps to heaven?'

'Yes,' Spider answered. Then he realised the female voice was a recording.

'Before we begin we need to confirm your age. If you are over eighteen, please answer "yes" now.'

'Yes.'

'We need a contact name and phone number. Please speak now.'

'Spider—I mean Sean O'Brien.' He rarely used his real name. Then he read out his mobile-phone number.

There was a click on the line. Then a male voice broke in.

'Welcome to *Kwizzers*. We will now ask you three questions. If you answer these questions correctly, you will be entered in the draw for Saturday night's show. Good luck.'

There was another click. Then the same male voice came back on the line, but with a slight echo, as if it had been recorded at a different time. Spider guessed there must be thousands of qualifying questions, randomly selected by computer.

'Question one: who was the last man to walk on the moon?'

Spider paused. Had the voice asked first man or last man? Last man, he thought. 'Ahem, the last man to walk on the moon was Gene Cernan. In 1972,' he added.

'Question two: name the Irish playwright who wrote *The Hostage*.'

Easy, Spider thought. 'Brendan Behan.'

'Question three: where were the 1936 Olympic Games held?'

Spider hesitated. Berlin or

London?

'Please indicate your answer.'

'Berlin,' he said decisively.

'Thank you for participating in *Kwizzers*. If you have answered correctly and are chosen by our computer, we will contact you. Good luck.'

The phone went dead.

9

'Gillian, you're eighteen. You don't know what love is,' Sarah Bradley said evenly. 'You're infatuated by Spider. But what sort of life could you build together? What sort of life would that be for a child?'

Gillian sat at the table and stared miserably at the slice of toast and the cup of slowly cooling tea. She'd spent a sleepless night asking herself the same questions. And she kept coming up with answers she didn't like.

Sarah sat opposite her daughter at the kitchen table. The house was quiet. Roy had gone to work. The two boys were in college. A radio talk show was whispering softly in the background.

Gillian looked up. 'Did you love Dad when you married him?'

Sarah sat back in the chair. The

quick answer was 'yes, of course I did'. But Sarah realised that Gillian might see through the lie. 'I liked him,' she said eventually. 'I liked him a lot.'

A ghost of a smile crossed Gillian's lips. 'But did you love him?'

'Loving and liking are two different things.' Sarah sipped her tea and nibbled at a triangle of toast. 'I knew he would make a good father. I knew he'd be a good provider, that he'd work hard, that he didn't drink. I liked him a lot, and, in time, we grew to love one another.'

'Was there someone you loved?'

Sarah was aware that the conversation she was having with her daughter was not one she could have had a month ago or a week ago. Then she'd looked on Gillian as a child. Now she was regarding her as a woman. She nodded. 'There was a boy. He was wild and handsome—so handsome. He wanted to marry me.

And I think I wanted to marry him. But it would have been a terrible marriage. We would have both ended up unhappy. It would have been cruel on the children too. He'd no job. He got casual work on the farms, but he had no prospects.'

'What happened to him?'

Sarah's smile was bitter. 'He got a girl into trouble, and they married. They ended up living in a caravan by the side of the road. The marriage lasted about a year. Then one day the girl took her child and walked out.'

'And the husband, where is he?'

'Still in the caravan by the side of the road. We pass it every time we drive to Galway,' Sarah said.

Gillian picked up her tea and sipped it. She made a face. It was cold.

Her mother got up to fill the kettle.

'You're saying I should have nothing more to do with Spider?'

Gillian said.

'I think you've got to consider your future and the baby's future—not just short term, but also long term. You've a bright future ahead of you. The baby is . . . a complication. But we can deal with that. I'm not sure how Spider fits into the picture, are you?'

Gillian bent her head and stared at the tea. Once it had been very clear: herself and Spider, married and happy together. They'd have a child in time, maybe even two, and a house of their own. But it had been a dream, nothing more. The reality was different: colder and harder.

*   *   *

They must have taken away her phone, Spider decided. He'd had no communication from Gillian for a couple of days. He was beginning to feel frantic.

He walked along the canal, head

bent. His phone was in his right hand, and he was using his thumb to tap in a message.

R U AROUND? MISSING YOU. THINGS OK?

He heard the ducks squawking behind him and glanced over his shoulder. He froze. Robert and Tony, Gillian's brothers, were racing down the path towards him. They had the same expressions on their faces as their father had had.

Spider turned and ran.

He walked this path every day. He knew its twists and turns. He could hear the two boys drawing closer. They were shouting at him, but Spider didn't listen. He knew if they caught up with him he'd get a beating or worse. They'd probably throw him in the canal. And Spider could not swim.

He leapt across a section of canal bank without breaking stride. Behind him he heard a shout and a splash. He risked a glance over his shoulder.

Tony had put his foot on a crumbling part of the bank, and his right leg had slid into the canal. His expensive jeans were black with foul water.

But Robert was gaining. He was probably the same age as Spider but at least a head taller and very broad. Spider knew that both brothers had been involved in martial-arts clubs.

Spider was coming up to the battered canal bench. Time, the elements and vandals had not been kind to it. He had an idea. He ran straight for the bench, jumped over the arm, lightly touched down on the seat and jumped off again. He was hoping Robert would follow him. He did.

Robert Bradley leapt over the arm of the bench. His foot landed heavily on the long slats of the seat. There was a crack, and the planks shattered. It sounded like gunshots. Robert's leg went straight through to the ground, trapping him.

Spider whooped, then cut away

from the canal and quickly lost himself in a maze of side streets. He was laughing and wheezing so hard that he almost didn't hear his phone ring.

'Yes?' he gasped.

'Is that Sean O'Brien?' The voice was soft and female.

'Yes?'

'Sean, you recently entered the qualifying round for *Kwizzers*.'

'Yes,' he gulped.

'I'm delighted to tell you that you've come through to the next round. Would you like to compete in this weekend's *Kwizzers* for a chance to win one million euro?'

Spider stopped. He swallowed hard. Suddenly his heart was thundering.

'Mr O'Brien, are you still there?'

'Yes. I'm just shocked—surprised.'

'We get that a lot,' the voice said. 'Take your time. Will you join us on Saturday?'

'Yes, of course. Yes.'

10

'Greg, I feel sick.'

'Me too,' Greg admitted, 'and I'm only sitting in the audience.'

The rest of the week had flown by. Spider had been in a daze for most of it. He'd tried to get hold of Gillian three or four times a day but without success. He'd called around to her house every night and lingered outside, hoping to catch a glimpse of her. He'd hung around the school and even spoken to some girls in her class, but they hadn't seen her. She was off sick.

He learned from Joey that Robert Bradley was in hospital. He'd snapped his ankle when he'd fallen through the bench. Long slivers of wood had been driven deep into his calf and thigh muscles, one of them coming dangerously close to his groin. Joey didn't ask how it happened, but he knew Spider walked down the canal every day coming to and from work. It didn't take a genius to work it out.

Kwizzers had been in touch with Spider twice: once to see if he wanted a lift to the studio and again to see if he was bringing any guests.

The only person he wanted to bring he couldn't get hold of, so he asked Greg. He realised Greg was the closest he had to a father figure. He also thought Greg would be a calming influence. As it turned out, Greg was even more nervous than he was.

They'd gone shopping on Friday afternoon, calling around to the Stephen's Green Shopping Centre. Greg advanced Spider some money, which he used to buy new black jeans and a plain white shirt. He also had new soles and heels put on his boots. Greg had then insisted that he get a hair cut. Spider wasn't sure. He viewed barbers the same way most

71

people regarded dentists. Finally he agreed, but only for a trim. When he sat in the chair and looked at himself in the mirror, he changed his mind and he came out of the barbers with a number four buzzcut.

Greg, who had been waiting outside, was shocked. He'd only ever seen Spider with long hair. 'New you, Spider?'

'New me, new beginnings. And if I win, a new start for Gillian and me.'

*   *   *

The studio was tiny.

When Spider had seen the show on TV the studio looked enormous. Now, with the cameras, lights and coils of cable everywhere, it looked small and cramped. He'd always imagined there would be hundreds of people in the studio audience. In reality, the studio could only hold around two hundred, including the contestants' guests.

When they'd arrived at the TV station, Spider and Greg were met by a young red-haired woman who'd introduced herself as Rachel. She was Spider's researcher, assigned to him for the day. If there was anything he wanted, all he had to do was ask.

She first took him into a small sitting-room, sat him down and went through a list of questions with him. One of the first questions she asked was if he had a criminal record. That would immediately disqualify him from the game.

Spider and Greg were then taken to the Green Room to meet the other contestants and relax before rehearsals.

As soon as they stepped into the Green Room, Spider and Greg spotted Harry Evans, the pub-quiz expert. His trademark comb-over was looking even more ridiculous than usual. It lay on his head like whipped cream on a bun.

Harry glanced across at the

newcomers and frowned. There was something familiar about them.

'You've got some competition,' Greg said. 'I recognise half a dozen of these guys from the pub-quiz circuit. And there's Harry of course.'

'Might as well go home if Harry's here,' Spider murmured.

'You'll do no such thing.'

'He'll remember us from the other night.'

'I doubt it. I'd have difficulty recognising you at the moment,' Greg said to Spider. 'You look . . . older somehow. It's the hair.'

'That and being a prospective father,' Spider added.

Rachel appeared at Spider's side. 'Is there anything I can get you?'

'We're fine,' Spider said.

'Here's what's going to happen. We'll have a bit of lunch now and a rehearsal this afternoon. Then we'll break for tea. The show goes out live at eight o'clock. Some people get very tired—it's the adrenalin—

so you might want to grab a nap. We advise against alcohol and sleeping tablets.' She smiled. 'Sometimes the effects take time to wear off.'

*　　　*　　　*

The rehearsal was a disaster.

The ten contestants were arranged in a long line of lighted seats. When they got a question wrong, the light went out over their seat. Then they were forced to sit there for the remainder of the programme. *Kwizzers* was an all-or-nothing show. There were no consolation prizes. You couldn't back out with your winnings at any stage during the game. You either went to the million or you left with nothing. Everyone there knew that, but many people played just to see how far up the scale they could go. There was no shame in losing a ten thousand or a hundred thousand euro question.

Spider got the second question

wrong, the ten euro question.

Kwizzers was hosted by Chip Walker, one of the new generation of radio hosts who had made the crossover to TV. Chip had actually introduced a version of *Kwizzers* on his drive-time radio show. Its success was one of the reasons the station had picked up the TV version.

Chip asked Spider a question. Although Spider could see Chip's mouth moving and hear the words, he couldn't make sense of them. His mind went blank. He was finally forced to shake his head and pass.

'Not to worry,' Chip said. 'This is only the rehearsal. It'll be all right on the night.'

Harry Evans won the rehearsal game, answering all of the questions correctly.

*   *   *

'I don't want to do it.' Spider stood before the mirror in the dressing-room and looked at his reflection. 'I'll make a fool of myself.'

The problem was that he had known the answers to the questions the other contestants had been asked. He had also known the answers to his own questions. He just hadn't been able to get the words out to answer them correctly. All he could think about was the money, how desperately he needed that million and how it would change his and Gillian's lives.

Rachel knocked at the door and popped her head inside. 'Hey, you look great. We'll be taking you down in about ten minutes. Is everything OK?'

Spider swallowed. 'Nerves.'

Rachel stepped into the room. 'Every contestant feels the same way.'

'Bet you Harry doesn't.'

'Well, maybe not him,' she agreed. 'But then he's got that comb-over to think about . . .'

Spider grinned.

'That's better. Look, the only advice I can give you is to pretend that this is just another pub quiz with a twenty-five euro prize. Try to stay in the moment. Don't think about what might happen, because it probably won't.'

'That's good advice. Thank you.'

'You'll do well tonight,' Rachel said and slipped out of the room.

Spider patted his back pocket and realised that he'd left his mobile in it. Automatically, he looked at the screen.

ONE MISSED CALL.

He thumbed the menu.

GILLIAN.

Spider's heart leapt. He looked for the time stamp on the call: two hours ago, when he'd been in rehearsals. He dialled 171, but there were no voice messages. He hit redial, not expecting to get a response . . . and got straight through.

'I've been so worried. Is everything

78

all right?'

'As right as it can be.' Gillian's voice sounded flat and tired.

'How are you feeling?'

'I'm OK.'

'Can we meet?'

'No, I don't think so.'

'Oh, I don't mean tonight. You'll never guess where I am. I'm going to be on *Kwizzers*. I'm going to try and win the million. Then there's no way your folks will be able to keep us apart.'

'Spider,' Gillian said very quietly, 'I don't think we should see one another again.'

'No!'

'Yes.'

'Gillian, please don't do this.'

'I've thought about this a lot. I've thought about nothing else. I want to go on with my life. I want you to go on with yours.'

'But I love you, Gillian.'

'I love you too, Spider. But I won't marry you. I can't marry you.'

'I'm going to win the million tonight—'

'It'll make no difference. I don't want to be with you. You're a dreamer, Spider. You'll always be a dreamer. I need more than that. Good bye.'

The phone went dead.

There was a knock on the door and Rachel looked in. 'Show time.'

11

The first thing that hit him was the smell. Two hundred people were crammed into a small room. The dozens of perfumes, body sprays and deodorants, mingling with the faintest hint of BO, gave him an instant headache.

Spider was numb. Gillian's words kept going round in his head. Even if he won the million, it didn't matter.

A not-very-funny warm-up comedian was going through an old routine to entertain the audience when the contestants were led out onto the stage. There were six men and four women. Harry Evans was smirking like a cat who'd got the cream. Greg had told Spider earlier that he'd overheard the crew betting that Harry would win. Spider glanced at him and couldn't resist a smile. With the overhead lights shining through his comb-over, it looked as if he was wearing a fuzzy cap.

The contestants were fitted with microphones and warned that everything they now said could be heard in the gallery. Then they were taken to their places in the line. Spider was third. Harry was tenth.

And then things began to move in a blur of speed.

The distinctive *Kwizzers* theme began. Chip Walker bounded out onto the set. He was wearing a white dinner jacket that threw back the light blindingly.

'Good evening ladies and gentlemen, and welcome to tonight's live edition of *Kwizzers*. We have ten new contestants tonight, each one ready to take seven steps to heaven. Let's introduce them . . .'

*   *   *

On the other side of the city, in a hospital room, the Bradley's were watching the television. Robert was lying in the bed, a cage over his legs to keep the blankets away from the skin. He needed another procedure to remove a six-inch sliver of wood from his inner thigh. The doctors were talking about scarring. Roy and Sarah sat on either side of the bed, while Tony slumped in boredom on the end of it. Gillian had the only chair.

Kwizzers was on the TV.

When Chip Walker introduced Sean O'Brien, it took her a moment to recognise him. When there were no comments from her family, she realised that they hadn't recognised him either.

He looks well, she thought. So handsome.

*   *   *

'You know the rules,' Chip said brightly. 'There are seven questions, the first worth one euro, the next worth ten, then one hundred, one thousand, ten thousand, one hundred thousand and finally one million. Is there a *Kwizzers* millionaire here tonight? Let's find out.'

The music thundered and suddenly the quiz show was underway.

*   *   *

Spider barely heard the questions. He kept repeating Gillian's words, trying to work out if she had been forced to say them. Perhaps her father or mother had been there when she'd taken the call. Maybe that was it. They'd been waiting for him to ring so she could use this carefully rehearsed speech.

But even as he was thinking it, he knew it wasn't true. Because he knew that Gillian had come to the same conclusion as him. What chance could he give a child? He had nothing.

'I'll need an answer.'

Spider blinked. 'I'm sorry, could you repeat the question?'

Chip smiled brightly, his teeth as white as his coat. 'Of course. How many strings has a mandolin?'

Spider breathed deeply. He glanced to either side and was shocked to discover that the only two lights left on were his and Harry Evans'. 'Eight,' he mumbled. Then again, more strongly, 'Eight, Chip.'

Chip paused for a count of ten, allowing tension to build. 'Eight it is. You've just won one hundred thousand euro.'

Someone in the audience screamed. Spider felt his stomach churn. Suddenly he needed—desperately needed—to go to the loo.

One hundred thousand euro. It was a huge sum. Yet without Gillian it was worthless to him.

'Harry, who is credited with writing "Home Thoughts, from the Sea"?'

Harry Evans looked blank. Spider stared at him. He had no idea of the answer.

Then Harry attempted a smile, which came out as a smirk. 'Robert Browning.'

Chip went through the charade of shuffling his cards, dragging out the tension. 'You're right. You've won one hundred thousand euro.'

The audience cheered.

Chip turned to face the camera. 'Well, this is a first. Two contestants are now about to go for the million euro question, about to take the seventh step to heaven. Will they make it? Come back after the break.'

The audience groaned.

As soon as the lights on the cameras went off, the make-up girls appeared. They began to pat down Spider and Harry, while another worked on Chip.

The tension in the studio was palpable. People were talking in whispers. Spider was aware that more and more people seemed to be gathering in the background. This was the first time in the run of the show that anyone had reached the million euro spot.

*   *   *

In the hospital bedroom the Bradley family were glued to the TV. 'That's a bright young man there,' Roy Bradley said. 'A million would set him up nicely. I could invest that for him, give him a good income for the rest of his life.'

Gillian opened her mouth to reveal Spider's identity, then said nothing.

*   *   *

'And you're back with us for the dramatic final part of *Kwizzers.*' Chip Walker was almost twitching with excitement. He was staring directly into the camera. 'Two contestants are going for the million euro question. We've never been here before. Even I'm not sure what happens next.' He swung around to face Spider and Harry. 'Lets play *Kwizzers*.' He looked from one to the other and finally settled on Harry. 'So, Harry Evans, the quiz master. You've set thousands of pub quizzes across the country. This must be easy for you?'

'Not that easy, Chip.' Harry smiled but kept his lips shut—he didn't want his yellowed dentures to appear on screen. When he won the million the first two things he was going to buy himself were a good wig and a new set of teeth. Maybe he'd even get hair implants. They were expensive but, hey, with a million he could well afford them.

'And you, Sean. I understand you're called Spider. Why is that?'

*   *   *

In the hospital room, Roy came slowly to his feet. He stepped up to the television and squinted at the grainy picture. Could it be? He glanced over his shoulder at his daughter and realised that it was indeed Spider.

'Still a bright young man, Dad?' she asked.

*   *   *

'Harry, we'll start with you. For one million euro: the character Berta appears in which opera?'

'*The Marriage of Figaro*,' Harry said instantly.

'Before we reveal the answer, we'll ask Sean his question. John Kelly, Grace Kelly's father, won a gold medal for rowing in which Olympic Games?'

And Spider suddenly realised he could win this million. He knew Harry's answer was wrong. Berta appeared in *The Barber of Seville*.

Greg jumped up from his seat,
cheering loudly. The audience went
wild. Streamers fell as Chip grabbed
Spider's hand and held it up high.